This edition published by Parragon Books Ltd in 2014 and distributed by

Parragon Inc.
440 Park Avenue South, 13th Floor
New York, NY 10016
www.parragon.com

ISBN 978-1-4723-6726-6

Printed in China

The Secret Garden

Based on the original story by
Frances Hodgson Burnett

Illustrated by

Laura Wood

PaRragon

Bath • New York • Cologne • Melbourne • Delhi
Hong Kong • Shenzhen • Singapore • Amsterdam

Mary Lennox was the most disagreeable-looking child anyone had ever seen. She had been born in India and had always been ill. Her father was forever busy and ill himself, and her mother had not wanted a little girl at all. When Mary was born, her mother handed her over to be looked after by servants. As the servants always obeyed Mary, she became very selfish.

One hot morning, when she was nine years old, Mary woke to find an unfamiliar servant by her bedside. The woman would not bring Mary's Ayah, her usual nanny, and so Mary threw herself into a tantrum and hit and kicked the woman.

When no one would tell her anything, Mary wandered outside and played under a tree, pretending to make a garden. She heard her mother talking on the veranda with a young army officer. The disease cholera had broken out, and Mary's Ayah had just died. Later that same day, three more servants died, and all the others ran away in terror.

The next day, Mary hid in the nursery and was forgotten by everyone. The house grew more and more silent. Mary was standing in the middle of the nursery when a strange man opened the door. He was horrified to see her, but Mary was only cross.

"I am Mary Lennox. I fell asleep when everyone had the cholera. Why was I forgotten?" She stamped her foot.

"Poor little child!" he said. "There is nobody left to come."

In that strange way, Mary found out that she had neither father nor mother left. There was no one in the bungalow but herself.

She was sent by ship to England to live with her uncle, Mr. Archibald Craven, at Misselthwaite Manor. When they landed, the officer's wife who had looked after her on the ship was very glad to hand the cross little thing over to Mr. Craven's housekeeper, Mrs. Medlock. The housekeeper was a stout woman, with very red cheeks and sharp black eyes.

After the ship, they took a train for a very long time. Mary sat in her corner of the carriage looking bored and fretful.

"You are going to an odd place," Mrs. Medlock told her. "The house is six hundred years old and on the edge of the moor. There's near a hundred rooms in it. Mr. Craven won't trouble himself about you. Most of the time he goes away, and when he's here, he shuts himself up and won't let anyone see him. He's got a crooked back and was a sour young man till he married a sweet, pretty thing. Then she died— and now he cares about nobody. You mustn't expect anyone to talk to you much."

The train took such a long time that Mary fell asleep. She awoke to find Mrs. Medlock shaking her. They had stopped at a station, and a smart carriage stood waiting for them. It rattled through the dark, over wild land that had no trees or hedges.

At last, they stopped in front of a long, low house built around a stone courtyard. Mrs. Medlock led Mary to a room with a lit fire and some supper on the table.

"Well, here you are!" Mrs. Medlock said. "This room and the next are where you'll live—and you must keep to them. Don't you forget that!"

When Mary opened her eyes in the morning, a young housemaid was cleaning the fireplace. Out of the window, Mary could see a great stretch of land with no trees on it. It looked like an endless, dull, purplish sea.

"That's th' moor," said Martha, the housemaid, in what Mary thought was a very strange accent. "Does tha' like it?"

"No," answered Mary. "I hate it."

"That's because tha'rt not used to it," Martha said. "But tha' will like it."

"Who is going to dress me?" demanded Mary.

"Canna' tha' dress thyself?" Martha said.

"What do you mean? I don't understand your language," snapped Mary.

"I mean, can't you put on your own clothes?"

"No," answered Mary. "I never did in my life. My servants dressed me."

"Well," said Martha, "it's time tha' should learn. It'll do thee good to wait on thyself a bit."

Mary could scarcely stand this.

At first, Mary was not at all interested in Martha. But after a few minutes, she began to take notice as Martha talked about her home, her eleven brothers and sisters, and how they played all day on the moor.

"Our Dickon, he's twelve, and he's got a young pony. He found it on th' moor. And it got to like him, so it follows him about an' lets him get on its back. Dickon's a kind lad, an' animals like him."

Mary began to feel a slight curiosity about Dickon.

In the nursery, a table was set with a good-sized breakfast. But Mary ate only a little toast and some marmalade.

After breakfast, Martha told her to put on her coat and play outside.

"Our Dickon goes off on th' moor by himself an' plays for hours. That's how he made friends with th' pony."

Martha told her how to get to the gardens. She seemed to hesitate a second before she added that there was a garden that no one had been in for ten years—a garden that had been beautiful and full of roses, but was now locked up and forgotten.

"Why?" asked Mary, in spite of herself.

"Mr. Craven had it shut when his wife died. It was her garden. He locked th' door an' dug a hole and buried th' key. Now, out you go to play."

As Mary walked through the walled gardens, she could not help thinking about the garden that no one had been in for ten years.

She followed paths and went through doors until she saw an old man with a spade over his shoulder. He looked startled when he saw Mary.

"What is that?" said Mary, pointing to a green door.

"Another garden. There's another t'other side o' th' wall, an' there's th' orchard t'other side o' that."

Mary went through to the orchard. She could see the tops of trees above a wall and a bird with a bright red breast sitting on one of them. Suddenly, the bird burst into song. She walked back to the old man.

"I went in the orchard. There was no door into the garden over the wall. But there are trees there—I saw a bird with a red breast sitting on one of them."

The man whistled, and the bird landed near his foot.

"What kind of a bird is he?" Mary asked.

"Doesn't tha' know? He's a robin redbreast. And I'm Ben Weatherstaff. Art tha' th' little girl from India?"

Mary nodded. The gardener jerked his thumb toward the robin. "He's th' only friend I've got."

"I have no friends. Would you make friends with me?" Mary asked the robin.

"Why," Ben cried, "tha' said that almost like Dickon talks to *his* wild things."

The robin flew over the wall.

"He lives there," said Ben. "Among th' old rose trees."

"Rose trees?" said Mary. "I should like to see them. There must be a door somewhere."

"None as anyone can find, an' none as is anyone's business. Get you gone an' play. I've no more time."

Each day, Mary ate a little breakfast, and realized that if she did not go out she would have to stay in and do nothing—so she went out.

She hated the wind, but the fresh air filled her lungs and whipped red into her cheeks. Mary stayed out of doors nearly all day, day after day, and when she sat down to her supper at night she felt hungry. She was not cross when Martha chattered away, and rather liked to hear her. One windy night she asked Martha why Mr. Craven hated the garden so much. Martha told her that Mrs. Craven had died there ten years ago when a branch she used to sit on broke.

Mary looked at the fire and listened to the wind howling outside. But she began to hear something else.

"Do you hear anyone crying?" she asked.

"No," Martha answered. "It's th' wind. Sometimes it sounds like someone lost on th' moor an' wailin'."

"But listen," said Mary. "It's in the house."

"It is th' wind," said Martha stubbornly. But Mary did not believe she was telling the truth.

The next day the rain poured down and Mary spent the morning wandering about the house. She lost her way two or three times, but at last she reached her own floor again. Then she heard a cry.

She put her hand on the tapestry near her. It covered a door which fell open into a corridor. Mrs. Medlock was hurrying along it with a very cross look on her face. She pulled Mary away by the arm.

"I turned round the wrong corner," explained Mary. "And I heard someone crying."

"You didn't hear anything of the sort. You come along back to your own nursery or I'll give you a slap."

And she dragged Mary to her own room.

Mary sat on the rug, pale with rage.

"There was someone crying—there was!" she said to herself.

Two days later, Mary went back to the gardens and saw the robin hopping about, pecking things out of a pile of earth. He pointed at something almost buried in the soil—an old key! Mary uncovered it and hid it in her pocket when she went back to the house for lunch.

Next day, she said to the robin, "You showed me where the key was yesterday. Please show me the door today!"

Just then, a gust of wind blew aside some ivy, and Mary saw the knob of a door that had been closed for ten years. She put the key in, turned it slowly, and pushed hard on the door. Then she slipped through, shutting the door behind her.

She was standing inside the secret garden.

The high walls were covered with leafless rose stems matted together. The branches had run all over the trees, swaying together like curtains.

Mary felt as if she had found a world all her own. She saw the sharp, little, pale green shoots of growing plants and wondered if they might be crocuses or snowdrops or daffodils. The plants were so close together that some did not seem to have room to grow. So she took a sharp piece of wood and dug up the weeds and grass, clearing space until it was time for her lunch.

"I wish I had a little spade," Mary said to Martha at lunch. "Then I could dig somewhere and make a little garden."

Martha knew a shop that sold little garden sets and seeds. She helped Mary write to Dickon, asking him to buy them and bring them over—Mary had enough money of her own, as each week she was given a little by Mr. Craven.

Mary was beginning to like being outside; she no longer hated the wind. She worked and dug and pulled up weeds steadily every day.

One day, when Mary went outside, a boy was sitting under a tree playing a wooden pipe. On the trunk of the tree was a brown squirrel, and two rabbits sat nearby.

"I'm Dickon," the boy said. "And I know tha'rt Miss Mary."

He had brought the tools and seeds and asked where her garden was.

"Could you keep a secret?" she said. "I've stolen a garden. Nobody cares for it. Nobody ever goes into it."

She lifted the hanging ivy, and they passed through together. Dickon stood looking around him.

"I never thought I'd see this place," he said.

"Did you know about it?" asked Mary. Dickon nodded.

Then he showed Mary that the stems of the roses had green inside them, so they were still alive. They began to work harder than ever, and Mary was sorry when she heard the clock strike for lunch.

There was a surprise waiting for her when she returned to the house: Mr. Craven had come back and wanted to see her. Mrs. Medlock took her along the corridors to a part of the house she had not been in before. A man with high, crooked shoulders was sitting before the fire. He looked as if he did not know what in the world to do with her.

"Are you well?" he finally asked.

"Yes," answered Mary.

"Do they take good care of you?"

"Yes."

"You are very thin," he said. He looked at her closely. "Don't look so frightened. Is there anything you want?"

"Might I," quavered Mary, "have a bit of earth to plant seeds?"

"You can have as much earth as you want," he said. "When you see a bit you want, take it, child—make it come alive." He paused, then said, "Now, you must go. I am tired."

That night, Mary woke to a strange sound. "That isn't the wind," she whispered. "I am going to find out what it is. I don't care about Mrs. Medlock. I don't care!"

She crept down the shadowy corridors, led by the far-off crying, until she found a big room she had never been to before. A thin, pale boy lay in a bed.

"Are you a ghost?" he said in a frightened voice when she entered.

"No," Mary answered. "Are you?"

"No," he replied. "I am Colin Craven. Mr. Craven is my father."

No one had told Mary that Mr. Craven had a son.

Colin told her that he was always ill. "If I live, I may have a crooked back and be a hunchback like my father. But I shan't live," he said. "My mother died around the time I was born, and it makes my father wretched to look at me."

"He hates the garden because she died," said Mary, half speaking to herself.

"What garden?" Colin asked.

"Oh! Just ... just a garden she used to like," Mary stammered.

He made her tell him about India and about her voyage across the ocean. And he told her about himself—how everyone had to do what he said because being angry made him ill.

"How old are you?" he asked.

"I am ten," answered Mary, "and so are you, because, when you were born, the garden door was locked and the key was buried. And it has been locked for ten years."

"What garden door was locked? Where was the key buried?" he exclaimed.

"Mr. Craven locked the door," said Mary. "No one knew where he buried the key."

Colin said he would force the servants to take him there. But Mary knew that would spoil everything! She promised that she would find a way for them to go together—then it would stay a secret garden.

The next day, Mary crept back to see Colin. She told him all about Dickon: how he could charm foxes and squirrels and birds, and how he knew everything about the moor.

"I couldn't go on the moor," Colin said. "How could I? I am going to die."

Mary didn't like the way he talked about dying. He almost boasted about it. So she continued talking about the garden. They were laughing about Ben Weatherstaff and the robin, when Colin's doctor and Mrs. Medlock walked in. They jumped in alarm, but then Colin introduced Mary.

"She makes me better," he said.

And so Mary was allowed to see Colin from then on.

For a week, the weather was bad, but finally, the sky was blue. Mary flew downstairs and out to the secret garden. Dickon was already there, working hard. Mary was so happy to meet his fox cub and his tame crow, Soot, that she could hardly breathe. She told him about Colin.

"If he was out here, he wouldn't be watchin' for lumps on his back," said Dickon. "It'd be good for him. Us'd be just two children watchin' a garden grow, an' he'd be another."

When Mary went to see Colin later, he was angry. He said he would send Dickon away if he kept Mary from him.

"If you send Dickon away, I'll never come again!" she retorted. "You're the most selfish boy I ever saw."

"I'm not as selfish as you," snapped Colin, "because I'm always ill, and I'm going to die."

"You're not!" said Mary sourly. "You just say that to make people sorry."

"Get out of the room!" he shouted.

"I'm going," she said. "And I won't come back!"

In the middle of the night, Mary was awakened by dreadful screaming and crying. Just then, Colin's nurse came in and begged her to go to Colin. Mary raced along the corridor.

"You stop!" she shouted at Colin. "I hate you! Everybody hates you! You will scream yourself to death in a minute, and I wish you would!"

"I can't stop!" he sobbed.

"You can!" shouted Mary. "Half that ails you is temper!"

"I felt the lump," choked out Colin. "I shall have a hunch on my back and die!"

"There's nothing the matter with your horrid back!" contradicted Mary. "If you ever say there is again, I shall laugh!"

Mary demanded the nurse show her Colin's back.

"There's not a single lump there!" said Mary at last. "There's not a lump as big as a pin—except normal backbone lumps."

No one but Colin knew what effect those words had on him. Now that an angry, unsympathetic little girl insisted that he was not ill, he actually felt it might be true.

"Do you think ... I could ... live to grow up?" he said.

The nurse said that Colin's doctor had said he would probably live if he did not give in to temper and if he spent time in the fresh air.

Colin's tantrum had passed, and he was weak with crying. He put out his hand toward Mary.

"I'll … I'll go out with you, Mary," he said, "if Dickon will push my chair. I do so want to see Dickon and the fox and the crow."

Mary looked at his poor, tired face, and her heart relented. She talked about the garden and Dickon until Colin fell asleep.

The next morning, Mary ran to Colin's room.

"It's so beautiful!" she said. "Spring has come! There are flowers uncurling and buds on everything—and Dickon has brought the fox and the crow and the squirrels and a newborn lamb!"

Dickon came into the room with the newborn lamb in his arms. The little fox trotted by his side, a squirrel sat on his left shoulder, and Soot on his right. Colin stared with wonder and delight. Dickon put the newborn lamb on Colin's lap, and it immediately turned to the warm, velvet dressing gown and began to nuzzle into its folds.

"I brought it a bit hungry because I knew tha'd like to see it feed," Dickon said. He took a feeding bottle from his pocket. Colin poured out questions, and Dickon answered them all, telling him about the flowers in the garden, too.

"I'm going to see them," cried Colin. "I am going to see them!"

"Aye, that tha' must," said Mary, quite seriously, in Dickon's accent.

One afternoon, Dickon pushed Colin's wheelchair to the
ivy-covered walls of the secret garden.

"This is where the robin showed me the key," said Mary. "And
here is the door! Dickon, push him in quickly!"

Little green leaves had now crept over the walls and trees, and
in the grass were splashes of gold and purple flowers. The sun fell
warm on Colin's face.

"I shall get well!" he cried. "And I shall live forever and ever!"

Mary and Dickon worked, and Colin watched. They
brought him things to look at: buds
that were opening, the feather of
a woodpecker, an empty eggshell.
Every moment was full of new things.

"I don't want this afternoon to end," he said, "but I shall come back. I'm going to see everything grow here, and grow here myself!"

They were quiet for a while, then Colin exclaimed, "Who is that man?"

Ben Weatherstaff was glaring at them over the wall from the top of a ladder!

He shook his fist at Mary and shouted at her. "I never thought much o' thee! Always askin' questions an' pokin' tha' nose where it wasna' wanted."

But when he spotted the wheelchair, he stopped shaking his fist and stared, open-mouthed.

"Do you know who I am?" demanded Colin.

Ben Weatherstaff passed his hand over his eyes.

"Aye," he said, "tha'rt th' poor cripple."

"I'm not a cripple!" Colin cried furiously.

Dickon held Colin's arm; the thin legs were out; the thin feet were on the grass. Colin was standing upright—as straight as an arrow!

Mary turned pale. "He can do it! He can do it!" she whispered to herself.

Ben Weatherstaff choked, and small tears ran down his cheeks.

"Eh! Th' lies folk tells!" he cried.

Colin made Ben Weatherstaff promise to keep their secret. Then Ben helped Colin to plant a rose.

"This is my garden now," Colin said, "and I shall come here every day."

Month after month, the garden grew more beautiful, and Colin grew stronger. One day, they all agreed that Dickon's mother, Susan Sowerby, could share the secret.

"It was a good thing that little lass came to th' manor," she said. "It's been th' savin' o' Colin. What do they make of it at th' manor?"

"They don't know," answered Dickon. "If the doctor knew, he'd write and tell Mester Craven, and Colin wants to show him hisself."

She laughed when they told her about their difficulty in pretending Colin was still a fretful invalid.

"Tha' won't have to keep it up much longer," she said.

During the months that the secret garden was coming alive, Archibald Craven had been traveling in faraway places. One morning, he had a letter from Susan Sowerby, asking him to come home.

In a few days, Mr. Craven was back at the manor house.

When he arrived, Mrs. Medlock told him that Colin was outside. Mr. Craven went through the gardens and found himself at his wife's favorite place. The ivy hung thick over the door, and yet there were sounds inside the secret garden like the laughter of children. And then feet ran faster and faster, and the door in the wall was flung wide open. A boy burst through it at full speed and dashed almost into his arms.

He was a tall boy and a handsome one, glowing with life. He threw the thick hair back from his forehead and lifted a pair of strange, gray eyes. It was the eyes that made Mr. Craven gasp.

"Who? What? Who?" he stammered.

"Father," he said, "I'm Colin. I see you can't believe it. I scarcely can myself! It was the garden that did it—and Mary and Dickon and the creatures. No one knows. We kept it to tell you when you came."

He said it all so much like a healthy boy that Mr. Craven shook with joy.

"Aren't you glad? I'm going to live forever and ever and ever!" said Colin.

Mr. Craven put his hands on the boy's shoulders.

"Take me into the garden, my boy," he said at last. "And tell me all about it."

The place was a wilderness of autumn gold and purple and violet-blue and flaming scarlet. Late roses climbed the trees, and hung clustered in the sunshine. Mr. Craven looked around and around.

Then they sat down under a tree—all but Colin, who wanted to stand while he told the story.

Archibald Craven thought it was the strangest thing he had ever heard.

"Now," Colin said, "it need not be a secret anymore. I am never going to get into that chair again."

When Mrs. Medlock looked out of the window, she shrieked. All the servants came running to see. There was Mr. Craven and, by his side, walking as steadily as any boy in Yorkshire, Master Colin. Following closely behind them was Mary, the most agreeable-looking child anyone had ever seen.